INTO
the
BIN
(and out again)

I2866697

Anne Fine

INTO the BIN
(and out again)

With illustrations by
Vicki Gausden

Barrington Stoke

For Gerry, with love

First published in 2019 in Great Britain by
Barrington Stoke Ltd
18 Walker Street, Edinburgh, EH3 7LP

www.barringtonstoke.co.uk

Text © 2019 Anne Fine
Illustrations © 2019 Vicki Gausden

The moral right of Anne Fine and Vicki Gausden to be
identified as the author and illustrator of this work has been
asserted in accordance with the Copyright, Designs and
Patents Act, 1988

A CIP catalogue record for this book is available
from the British Library upon request

ISBN: 978-1-78112-858-9

Printed in China by Leo

Contents

Chapter 1

"Mess, mess and more mess!"

Mrs Carter, the head teacher, was not at all happy. She made Mr Frost's class stay back at the end of Friday Assembly so she could tell them off.

"I just walked into your class's cloakroom and what did I see? Pencils and felt-tip pens on the floor. Shoes and books and gloves and old worksheets lying about. Mess, mess and more mess!"

Mrs Carter shook her head. "It won't do! We can't have all these odd things lying about. People will trip and hurt themselves. You must keep the floor clear and tidy. You are all going to have to make more of an effort."

Almost everyone felt bad. They knew Mrs Carter was right. The problem was that most of them were always in a hurry. In the morning, they were rushing to take off their coats and find their friends. At break, they were keen to get outside to play. By lunch-time, they were hungry and wanted to get to the front of the dinner line.

And at the end of the day, of course, everyone was in a hurry to go home.

Mrs Carter pointed to the hall doors. "Off you go," she said. "Back to your classroom. And don't forget that from today we are all going to fight the great battle against mess, mess and more mess!"

Chapter 2
"Stupid, stupid bin!"

Back in the classroom, Mr Frost wrote the date on the board. Then he turned round. The side of his foot knocked the waste bin and it tipped over. Rubbish spilled over the floor.

Everyone at the front heard him mutter, "That stupid, stupid bin!"

"It's too light," Georgia explained, "because it's made of tin."

"It gets knocked over all the time," said Alfie. "You only have to breathe and over it goes."

"That's the third time this week," said Petra. She got up to help Mr Frost pick up the tissues and snack wrappers and bits of string, and drop them back in the bin.

At the back of the room, Mohammed chuckled. "That bin isn't just *full* of rubbish," he told everyone. "That bin *is* rubbish."

Mr Frost gave a sigh. "Mohammed's right," he said. "This bin is rubbish. I'm sick of it. This weekend I'm going to buy a big wooden one that will never tip over." He scowled. "And I'll chuck this stupid thing into the wheelie bin at the school gate."

"That would be a terrible waste," said Tara. "There's nothing really *wrong* with the waste bin. It's a lovely bright-red colour."

"Nice and shiny," agreed Logan.

"With only one tiny scratch," added Ethan, "that no one would even see if it was in a corner."

"My mum can take it to her charity shop," said Georgia. "Someone will buy it."

"It's a big bin to carry all the way to your house," warned Ethan. "Almost as big as a skip."

"What's a skip?" Alysha asked.

"One of those rubbish things so big a lorry brings it and dumps it on the side of the street."

"Then all the neighbours sneak out at night to put in stuff they don't want any more," Safi told her.

"And other neighbours sneak out after that to take the things they fancy back out again," Mohammed joked.

"We could do that," said Martha. "We could put stuff we don't want into Mr Frost's bin before it goes."

"Don't bring in rubbish!" Georgia warned. "The charity shop won't want a bin full of rubbish!"

"No," said Mohammed. "They'll just want the rubbish bin!"

They were still laughing when the bell rang for the end of the day.

Chapter 3

"I hate her and I want her gone!"

On Monday morning, Safi, Petra and Alfie came in with plastic bags and Logan had a box. He carried it so slowly and carefully that he took ages to get across the classroom.

He put the box down almost without breathing. He set a chair under the highest shelf. Everyone watched as he picked up the box, climbed on the chair and, oh, so slowly and gently, slid it onto the shelf.

"Phew!" he said. "Phew! I got it up there without setting it off!"

Petra stared. "Is it a bomb?"

"Of course not," Logan said. "It's just some old toy I'm going to put in the bin."

"You didn't *carry* it as if it were just some old toy," Petra said.

Logan made a face. "Well, you don't *know* it, do you?" he said.

He was about to explain but Mr Frost walked in.

He was carrying a splendid new waste bin. It was big. It was square. It was wooden. It was solid.

"Ta-*da!*" he said proudly.

"Is it as heavy as it looks?" asked Paul.

Mr Frost dumped the new bin on the floor beside his desk. "Very heavy," he said, and gave the bin a hefty kick. It didn't even skid across the floor, let alone fall over.

"That's good," said Alfie. "That bin will definitely suit us better."

Mr Frost picked up the bright red shiny tin
waste bin that only had one tiny scratch.

"Right," he said. "Who wants to put
something in this one before it goes?"

Four hands went up. Safi's waved madly. "Can I be first?" she begged. "I can't wait to be rid of this cat!"

"What cat?" asked Mr Frost.

Safi dipped in her bag and brought out the most wonderful china cat. It was life-sized, with pert ears and slanted eyes. Beautiful

orange streaks ran down its glossy china fur.
Its paws were neat little circles.

The china cat was perfect. Perfect!

"You can't give that away," said Logan.

"I can," said Safi. "And I will. I hate her and
I want her gone!"

The whole class stared at the china cat. Then they stared at Safi.

"She looks so *real*," breathed Ethan.

"*Too* real," said Safi. She turned the cat round so everyone could see. "She has the weirdest, scariest eyes and she is always watching. Staring all the time."

Everyone left their desks to gather round the cat. Even Mr Frost came to take a closer look.

"They are very scary eyes," admitted Paul. "And I'm not one to freak out easily."

"Neither am I!" snapped Safi. "No one could feel safe with this cat staring at them."

Everyone stared at the cat some more. The cat stared back. After a moment, Tara said, "I wouldn't want that cat staring at me. I might even choose to *smash* her."

At once, Mr Frost reached out for the cat and carried it to the bin. He was about to put it in when Alysha put up her hand.

"Can I have Safi's scary china cat, please?"

Mr Frost was startled. "You really want it, Alysha?"

"Yes," Alysha explained. "You see, I have
a little garden of my own at home, and that
cat is the perfect thing to put down where I've
planted seeds. She'll scare the birds away."

"She'd scare off *anything*," said Ethan. "Your plants will definitely be safe!"

"Is that OK?" Mr Frost asked Safi.

Safi nodded. So Mr Frost handed the cat to Alysha. "There you go," he said. "One scary cat for Alysha's garden. Now who wants to be next?"

Chapter 4

"But you promised me!
You *promised* me!"

"I'm next," said Alfie. He waved his bag. There didn't seem to be anything in it. It might even have been empty.

"Before I show you what I'm putting in the bin," he said, "I need to explain. It's not like Safi's cat. It's not the thing itself that I can't stand. In fact, I really like it."

Paul asked, "So why put it in the bin?"

"I can't stand how it makes me *feel*," said Alfie. He made a face. "You see, it all began when I was with my nana." He looked around the class. "You know my nana, don't you?"

They all did.

"Your nana who waits for you almost every day at the gates?"

"And takes you swimming on Tuesdays?"

"And watches you for hours at the skate park?"

"And walks your puppy when your mum's at work?"

"The nana who rushed back to your house to get your pirate costume for the play when you forgot it?"

Alfie hung his head. "Yes," he admitted. "That nana."

Everyone waited. Alfie's silence went on for ages. In the end, Mr Frost had to say, "Come on, Alfie. Tell us the story."

Alfie took the deepest breath. "It was like this," he said. "I'd had a cold for four whole days, and Nana looked after me. She was so nice. We played a thousand board and card games. She let me watch telly. She read me half a billion books."

"Not half a billion," said Petra. "By the time she finished, you'd be an old man with a beard down to your feet."

"A hundred then," said Alfie. "She was so good to me. She cooked my favourite meals and didn't mind if I couldn't finish them. She made sure my hot water bottle was always warm. She fluffed up my pillows. She—"

Mr Frost broke in. "We've got the idea, Alfie. Your nana is a saint. Let's get on with the story."

"So I got better," Alfie said. "But two days later, when Nana and I were in the supermarket, Nana suddenly said that she felt terrible – all cold and shivery, with blurry eyes and a head full of steel hammers."

"She'd caught your cold," said Logan.

Alfie nodded. "It was so bad she couldn't push the trolley. I took it to the checkout. And that's when I remembered that while I was still in bed, she'd cheered me up by promising me a box of Sugar Noddles."

"Why did you want Sugar Noddles?" asked Georgia. "They're not even very nice. They're gritty and they taste too much of nuts."

"I didn't really want the Noddles," Alfie admitted. "I wanted the free dragon gift inside

the cereal pack." He hung his head again, remembering. "I made the most shocking fuss. It was almost a tantrum. I kept on shouting at Nana, 'But you promised me! You *promised* me!' till all the other shoppers stared. But Nana felt too weak and rotten to be firm with me, like she'd have been on any other day. She was too ill to tell me off."

Alfie sighed at the awful memory. "So I dragged my poor nana back down the aisles, looking for Sugar Noddles, even though I knew she was desperate to get home."

Everyone watched Alfie carefully. He was almost in tears as he told his sad story.

"And when we found the Noddles, there were no more boxes with the dragon gift. I didn't even stop then! I forced Nana to ask an assistant, and we had to wait for ages while he went to the storeroom at the back to find a Sugar Noddle box that had the dragon."

Alfie's face was red with shame. "And only then did I let Nana go to the checkout and take me home."

There was a long, long silence. Then Mr Frost said, "All right, Alfie. Let's see this Sugar Noddle dragon that makes you feel so awful that you want to give it away."

Alfie reached in his bag and drew out a tiny green plastic dragon. It was so small that some people in the class had to come closer to even see that it was there.

"Right," Mr Frost said. "Come up and put it in the bin."

Alfie walked up to the front and dropped the tiny green dragon in the big red shiny waste bin.

"Phew!" he said. "I am so glad to see the back of that."

As he walked back to his desk, smiling happily, Sarah rushed past him.

"Can I have the dragon, please? Oh, please! You see, I've been trying to knit a kangaroo." She blushed. "The problem is that my knitting's gone wonky and the kangaroo looks more like a dragon." She picked Alfie's tiny dragon out of the bin. "And this would be perfect for a dragon baby. I can put it in the little pouch I knitted on the front of my dragon when she was still a kangaroo."

Sarah beamed at Mr Frost. "Oh, please say I can have it!"

"That's up to Alfie," said Mr Frost.

Alfie gave a shrug. "Sure! She can have the dragon so long as when I'm around he's tucked so deep down in the pouch that I don't have to see him."

"Perfect," said Mr Frost. He handed the dragon to Sarah. "So who's next?" he asked.

Chapter 5

"I was scared of the sun."

"Me," Petra said. She pulled a book out of her bag. "This is what I'm putting in. It's the best book I've ever read and it's called *How to Stop Worrying*."

"Why are you giving it away?" Ethan asked her.

"Because I don't need it any more," said Petra. "And it might help somebody else."

"How did it help you?" persisted Ethan.

Petra blushed. "I was scared of the sun."

More than one person giggled.

"Scared of the sun?" said Ethan. "How can anyone be scared of the sun? Did you think it would drop down and bite you? Were you scared you might touch it by mistake and burn your fingers?"

"Nothing like that," said Petra. "But when I was only three, my uncle told me that if you look at the sun, you go blind."

"You do have to be careful," Mr Frost warned. "Staring at the sun can hurt your eyes."

"I know that *now*," said Petra. "But I was only *three*. I thought that if you even looked at the sun for a second, you would go blind. I got upset if I was sent outside on sunny days. And if they took me for a walk, I didn't look up. Not ever."

"You didn't look up? Not at all?"

"No," Petra told them. "I wouldn't even bounce on my trampoline or spin round in circles in case I made a mistake and opened my eyes when the sun was in front of me."

Mr Frost asked Petra gently, "So how did the book help?"

"Simple," said Petra. "The book explains that most worries are because you heard something wrong or were told something silly. It said you had to *ask*."

"Just that?" Mohammed said. "Just that you had to *ask*?"

"Yes. Just that. So I made a list of all the things I worried about and took it to my mum and dad to ask them."

Mohammed asked, "Were all your other worries silly too?"

"No!" Petra told him crossly. "One or two were quite sensible."

Everyone wanted to know more. "Which? Which sensible worries did you have?"

"Mind your own business," snapped Petra. "My worries are private, thank you."

"Quite right," said Mr Frost.

"All I'm going to say," said Petra, "is now I know to *ask*. So I want someone else to have the book and I hope it ends up with someone with a stupid worry like mine."

She'd only just put it in the bin when Paul rushed up from his desk.

"Can I take it?" he begged her. "My job at playtime is Friendship Monitor. Lots of the children who come to the Friendship Bench in the playground have terrible worries. This is the perfect book to share with them."

Petra took it out of the bin again and handed it over.

Mr Frost peered in the big red shiny tin waste bin. "Still empty," he told them. "And now there's only one more person to go."

Chapter 6

"Oh, stop it!
Mr Frost, just make it stop!"

Mr Frost told Logan, "Try to be quick, so we can get down to some work."

"It won't be up to me how quick we are," Logan said. "It'll be up to the thing I want to put in the bin."

He moved his chair to under the highest shelf and reached for his box. The moment he touched it, a noise started up inside. It was a

sort of grinding and chugging and hooting and
pipping.

"For heaven's sake!" said Mr Frost. "What
on earth's that?"

"It's my toy concrete mixer," Logan said. "I was given it years ago. Mum hid it in a cupboard."

"I'm not surprised," said Mr Frost. "That is the noisiest toy I've ever heard."

"It's miles louder out of the box," warned Logan.

The awful noise went on for quite a while and then it stopped.

"Why didn't your mother leave it in the cupboard?" Lily asked.

"She did," said Logan. "But when I was looking for my boots, I found it and made the mistake of putting in new batteries." One of his hands brushed the box. The frightful grinding and chugging and hooting and pipping began again.

"Oh, no!" said Mr Frost. "Don't keep on setting it off!"

"I didn't mean to," Logan defended himself. "You only have to breathe on it for it to start."

"Take out the batteries," said Paige.

"I can't," said Logan. "I jammed the cover back on wrong and now the batteries are stuck inside."

They waited till the awful noise had finished.

"What is the pipping, exactly?" Christy asked.

"I think it means, *This vehicle is reversing*," Logan explained.

"Take it out of the box," Ethan ordered. "Let's see this terrible noisy toy."

Mr Frost said, "I'm not sure that's a good id—"

But Logan had already lifted the lid. The noise began again but even louder.

Mohammed and Tara clapped their hands over their ears. "Oh, stop it! Mr Frost, just make it stop!"

"Yes," Mr Frost said. "Logan, make it stop!"

"I can't," wailed Logan. "It has to finish by itself."

He set the concrete mixer down. Everyone watched as it trundled back and forth across the table, chugging and grinding and hooting and pipping.

"I can see why your family want to give that away," said Mr Frost as soon as the room was quiet again.

"Someone will love it," said Logan. "It's far too good a toy to just chuck out."

"Far too good," said Mr Frost. "I *don't* think!"

As Logan carried the concrete mixer up to the front of the class, it started off again. Once it was inside the bin, it sounded even louder.

Suddenly, Lily jumped to her feet. "Give it to me!" she said. "I know a little boy who'll love that toy. His mum and dad are deaf. That toy won't bother them at all. But he will love it. Give it to me."

"All right," said Mr Frost. "But Logan must put it back on that high shelf until the end of the day. It'll be safer there."

"And so will we!" said Tara with a smile.

So, while the toy kept chugging and grinding and hooting and pipping, Logan climbed on the chair and slid it back on the high shelf.

When there was silence again, Mr Frost looked round the room. "Are we all done?" he asked.

Mohammed chuckled. "Everything into the bin – and out again! Just like a skip! Maybe the people who took those things should bring in something tomorrow, to make up."

"No!" Mr Frost said. "No, they should not! This is a classroom, not a recycling centre!"

He picked up the bright red shiny tin waste bin with only one tiny scratch and put it safely out of the way, in the corner. "This bin is going off with Georgia tonight," he told them. "Out of this classroom for *ever*."

Chapter 7

"Perfect, perfect lost-property bin!"

As soon as the bell rang at the end of the day, Mr Frost told them to get in line.

Alysha put her cat safely in her book bag so Safi didn't have to see its scary eyes.

Sarah kept the tiny green dragon deep in her pocket so Alfie didn't have to look at it.

Paul put the *How to Stop Worrying* book on the shelf so he could take it to the Friendship Bench the next day.

And Mr Frost picked up the chugging, grinding, hooting and pipping concrete mixer so none of the other teachers would tell Lily off for making too much noise. "I'm taking it out to the middle of the playground," he told her. "So it doesn't wake all the babies who've come with some of the parents to pick you up."

He went out of the school through the side door. The rest of them went down the corridor to the cloakroom, with Georgia carrying the big red shiny waste bin.

There was the usual mess all over the floor. Pencils and felt-tip pens. Shoes and books and gloves and old worksheets.

While they were putting on their coats, Mrs Carter came along to say goodbye to everyone. She looked at the floor and her face went red. "Look at it!" she told them. "Just look at it! Just like before! Mess, mess and more mess!"

Then she saw Georgia with the big red shiny waste bin in her arms. Mrs Carter asked Georgia, "Where's that from?"

"From our classroom," Georgia said. "But Mr Frost doesn't want it any more."

Mrs Carter's eyes lit up. "But it's a *wonderful* bin!" she cried. "It's big and red and shiny. And it only has one tiny scratch."

"Yes," Georgia told Mrs Carter. "It is a really good bin. That's why I'm taking it home. My mum will take it to her charity shop and it will go to someone who needs it."

Mrs Carter reached out for the bin. "Don't take it home," she begged. "Give it to me."

"Why?" Georgia asked. "Do you need a waste bin, Mrs Carter?"

"Not a waste bin," Mrs Carter admitted. "What I need is a tidy place to keep things."

"A lost-property bin!" cried Safi.

"That's right," said Mrs Carter. "A lost-property bin!"

She held out her arms again. "Yes! Give it to me, please, Georgia. It's just the job for fighting the great battle against mess. It's big, so all these things on the floor will fit inside it. It's bright and red and shiny, so everyone can see it. And it only has one tiny scratch."

"If you keep it in the corner," Ethan told her, "no one will see the scratch."

Mrs Carter said, "It is the perfect, perfect lost-property bin!"

So Georgia gave Mrs Carter the bin and Mrs Carter put it in the corner so the scratch was hidden. "Right!" she said. "Now, before you go home, I want this mess picked up off the floor."

Mohammed and Martha picked up the pencils and felt-tip pens. Petra and Ethan picked up the shoes and gloves. Alfie and Safi

picked up the worksheets. Logan picked up a
book.

They put everything carefully into the bin, so, in the blink of an eye, the floor was clear.

Mrs Carter was delighted. "See! And there's still room for more."

She said goodbye to everybody. Just as the last one had left, Mr Frost hurried in carrying another book. "Has Paul gone? I've just found this story on the Friendship Bench."

"Too late!" said Mrs Carter. "So just put the book into the bin."

"Into the bin?" Mr Frost was astonished. "But it's a perfectly good book! And someone might still be reading it."

"It's not that sort of bin any more," said Mrs Carter. She pointed. "See? Things will go in one day. They'll sit there neatly, then they'll come out again!"

Mr Frost saw the big red shiny bin in the corner, half full of felt-tip pens and shoes and gloves and worksheets.

"Perfect!" he agreed. "Just perfect. Into the bin, and out!"

They went back to the staffroom side by side, chuckling.

Our books are tested
for children and young people by
children and young people.

Thanks to everyone who consulted on
a manuscript for their time and effort in
helping us to make our books better
for our readers.

Also by Anne Fine ...

ISBN: 978-1-78112-285-3

ISBN: 978-1-78112-204-4

ISBN: 978-1-78112-243-3

"A superb and subtle writer"

MAL PEET, *THE GUARDIAN*